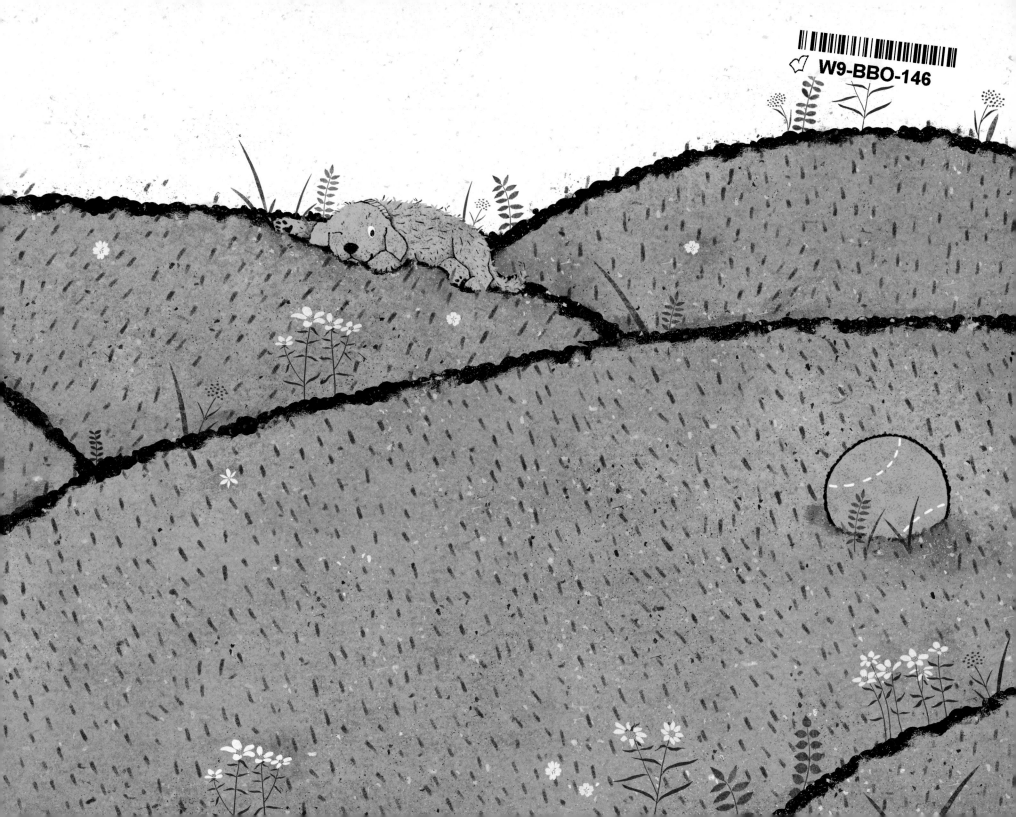

This Little Pup

laura j. bryant

Albert Whitman & Company
Chicago, Illinois

One blue ball...

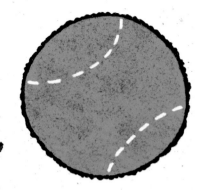

bounced past two brown cows.
Two brown cows...

spied three green frogs.

Three green frogs…

jumped over four pink pigs.

Four pink pigs…

rolled in the mud and

made a big mess!

Five white sheep giggled
and **six purple butterflies…**

fluttered away.

Seven orange kittens were on the hunt…

for a quiet place to nap. But it was not quiet!
Eight red birds were chirping…

and **nine black hens** were squawking...
because **ten yellow chicks** were missing!

OH MY!

Not to worry. They were over by the barn watching

one **blue ball...**

bounce…

and bounce...
and bounce...

until...

it was caught by **this little PUP!**

For my little pup, Izzy—LJB

Library of Congress Cataloging-in-Publication data is on file with the publisher.

Text and illustrations copyright © 2020 by Laura J. Bryant
First published in the United States of America in 2020 by Albert Whitman & Company
ISBN 978-0-8075-7865-0 (hardcover)
ISBN 978-0-8075-7864-3 (ebook)

Printed in China
10 9 8 7 6 5 4 3 2 1 WKT 24 23 22 21 20 19

Design by Laura J. Bryant and Aphelandra Messer

For more information about Albert Whitman & Company,
visit our website at www.albertwhitman.com.

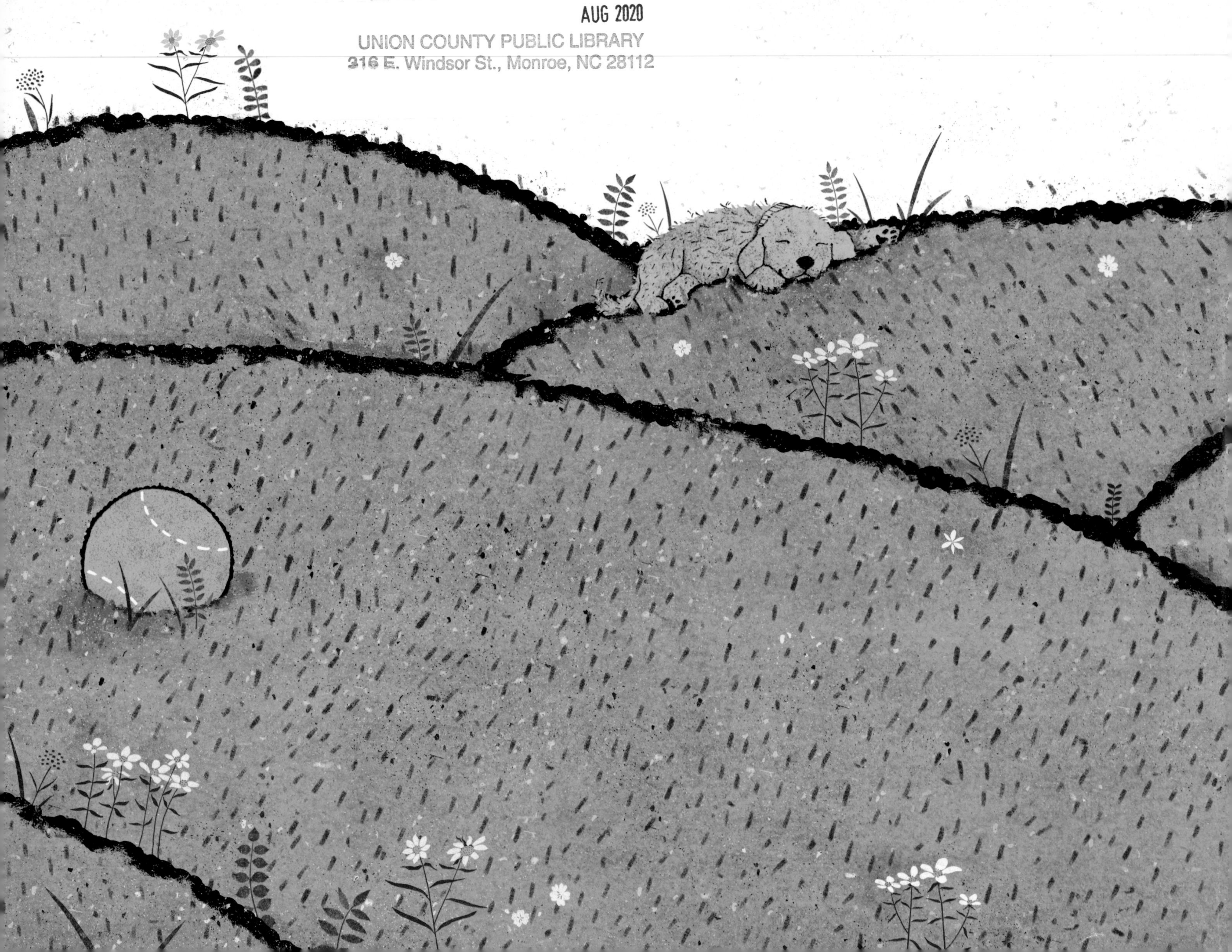